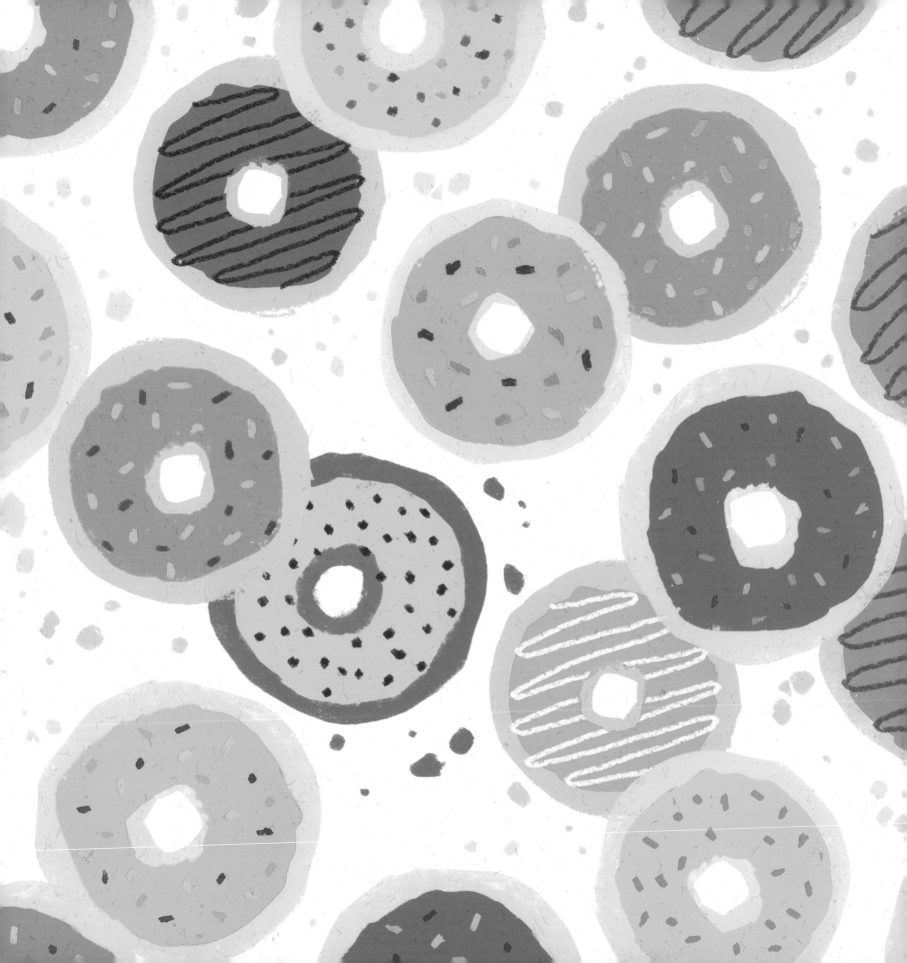

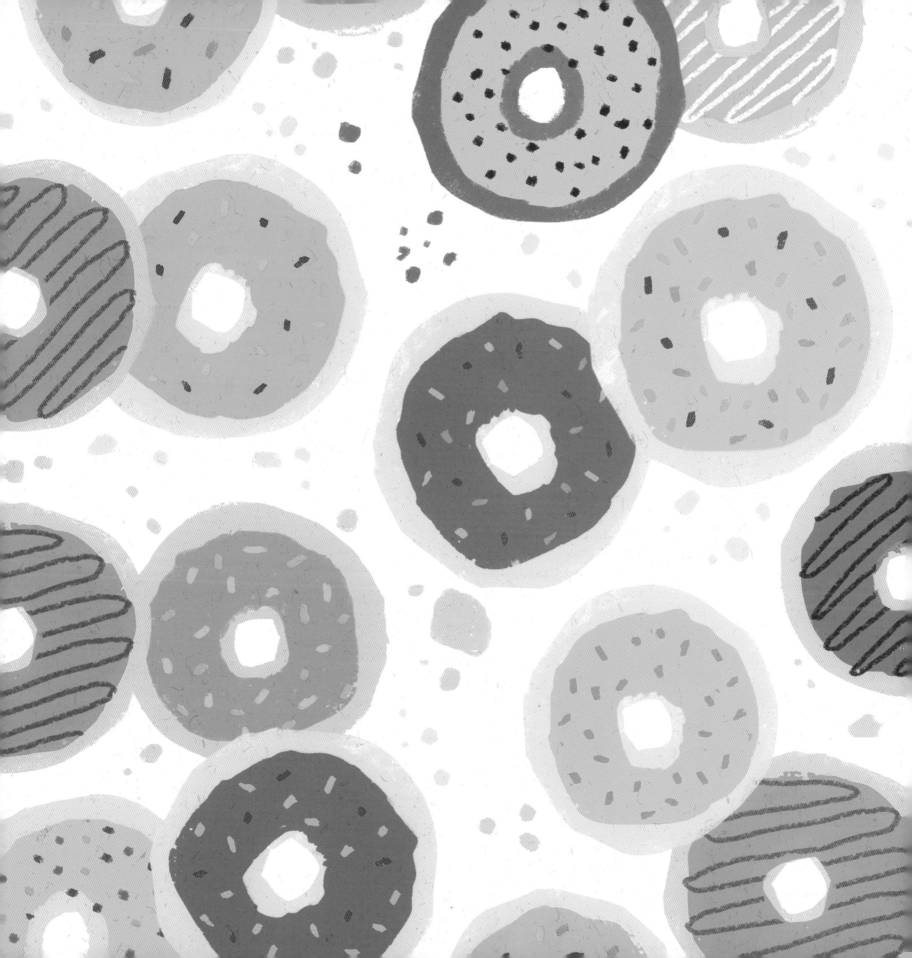

IMAGINE THAT

Licensed exclusively to Imagine That Publishing Ltd
Tide Mill Way, Woodbridge, Suffolk, IP12 1AP, UK
www.imaginethat.com
Copyright © 2021 Imagine That Group Ltd
All rights reserved
2 4 6 8 9 7 5 3 1
Manufactured in China

Written by Seb Davey
Illustrated by Alex Willmore

ISBN 978-1-80105-374-7

A catalogue record for this book is available from the British Library

For the roarsome 8. SD

DONUT TOUCH!

Written by
SEB DAVEY

Illustrated by
ALEX WILLMORE

This is Mikey ...

These donuts are **mine!**
Keep your fingers away from them ...

DO NOT
TOUCH!

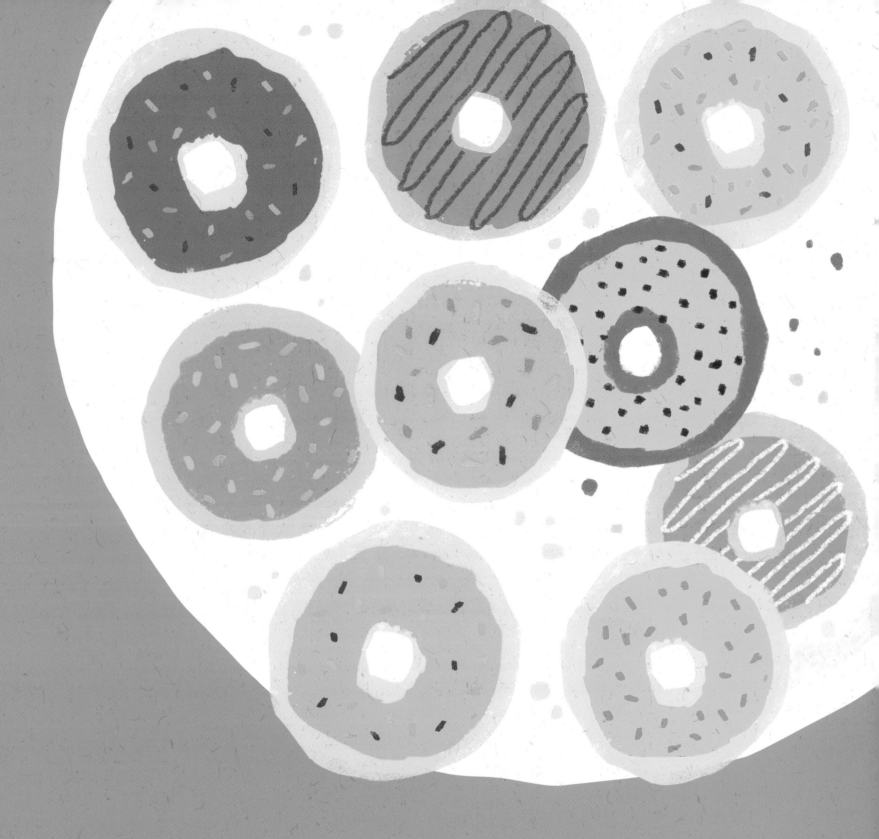

Don't upset Mikey! Turn the page
without touching the donuts.

Hey!
One of my
donuts is **missing!**

Did you touch my donuts?
Keep your fingers away
from them ...

**DO NOT
TOUCH!**

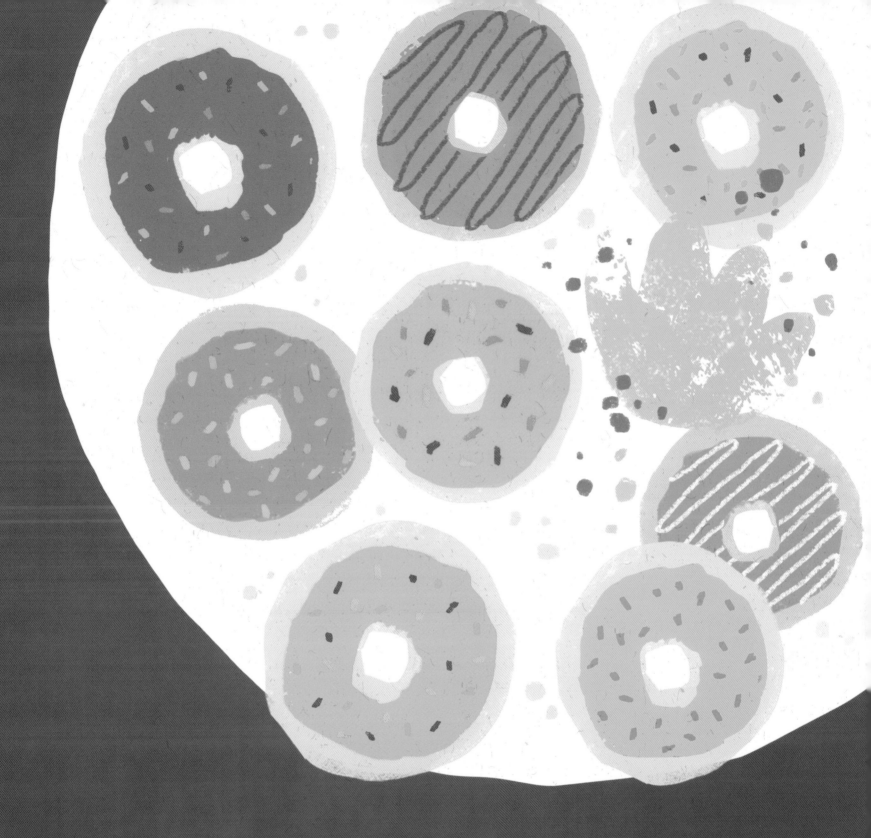

Mikey seems angry! Turn the page without touching the donuts. Be very careful!

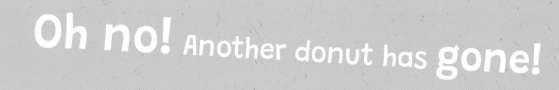

Oh no! Another donut has **gone!**

Did you touch my donuts?
Keep your fingers away from them ...

DO
NOT
TOUCH!

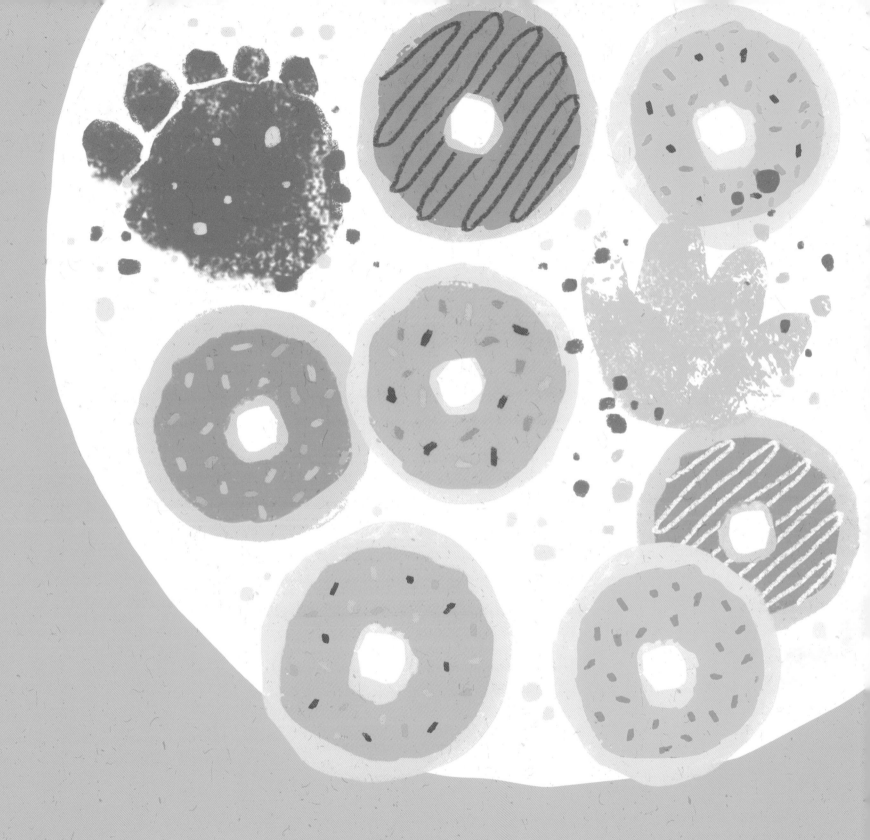

Mikey is really mad now! Turn the page without touching the donuts ... not even a crumb!

Woah!
A donut just
disappeared!

Did you touch
my donuts?
Keep your
fingers away
from them ...

DO
NOT
TOUCH!

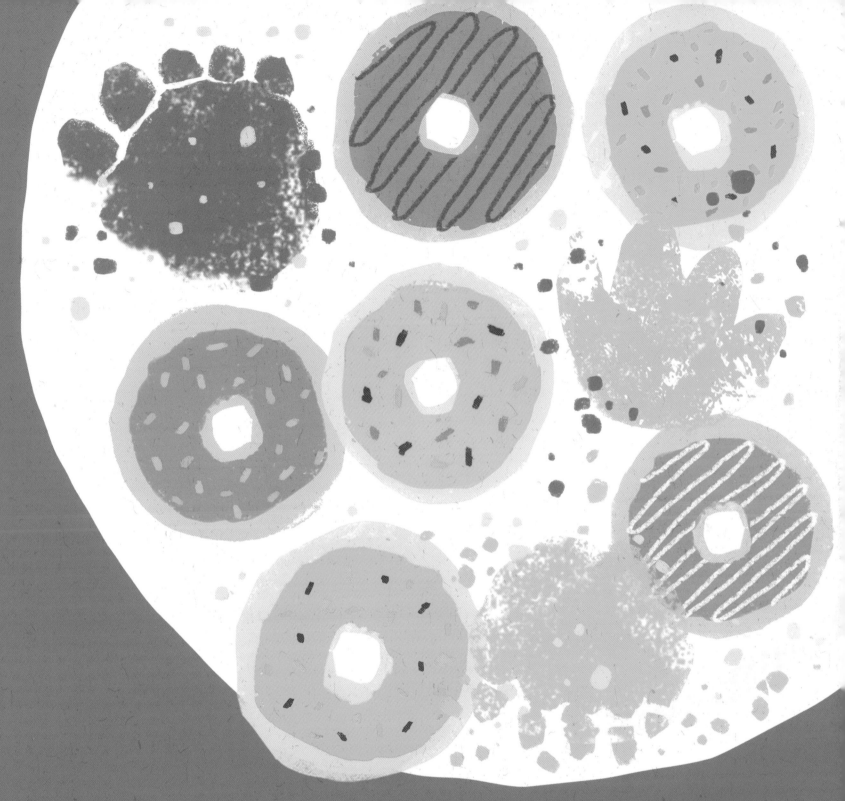

Uh-oh! Mikey thinks **you** have taken his donuts!
Turn the page without touching the donuts.
Mikey is watching you!

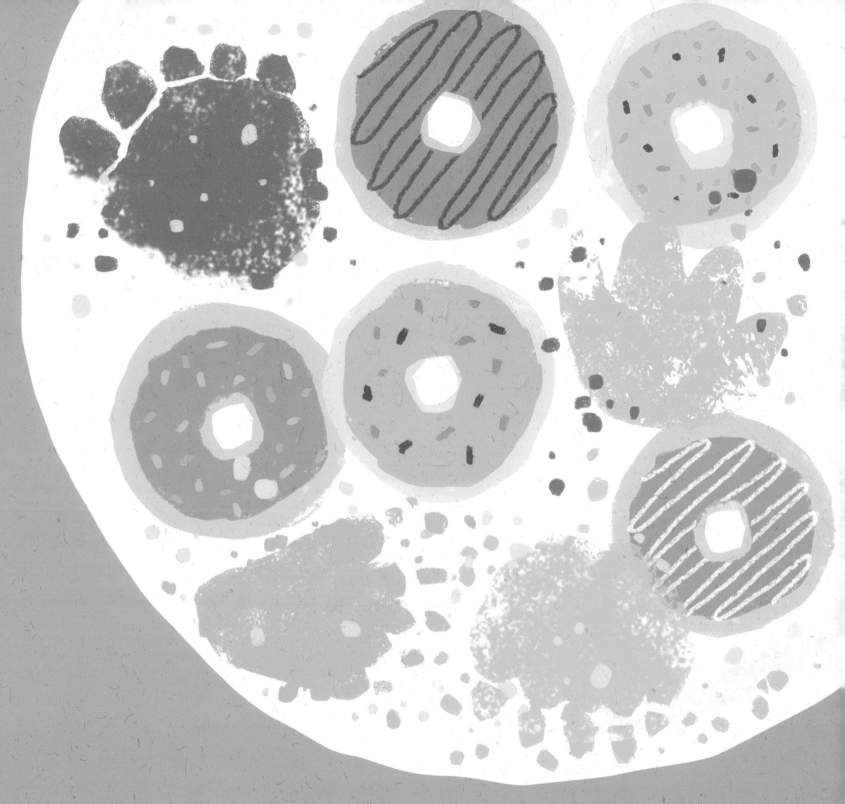

Who is taking Mikey's donuts?
Turn the page without touching the donuts ...
or the crumbs ... or the frosting!

Roar!
Even **more** donuts have vanished!

Did you touch my donuts?

Keep your fingers away from them ...

DO NOT TOUCH!

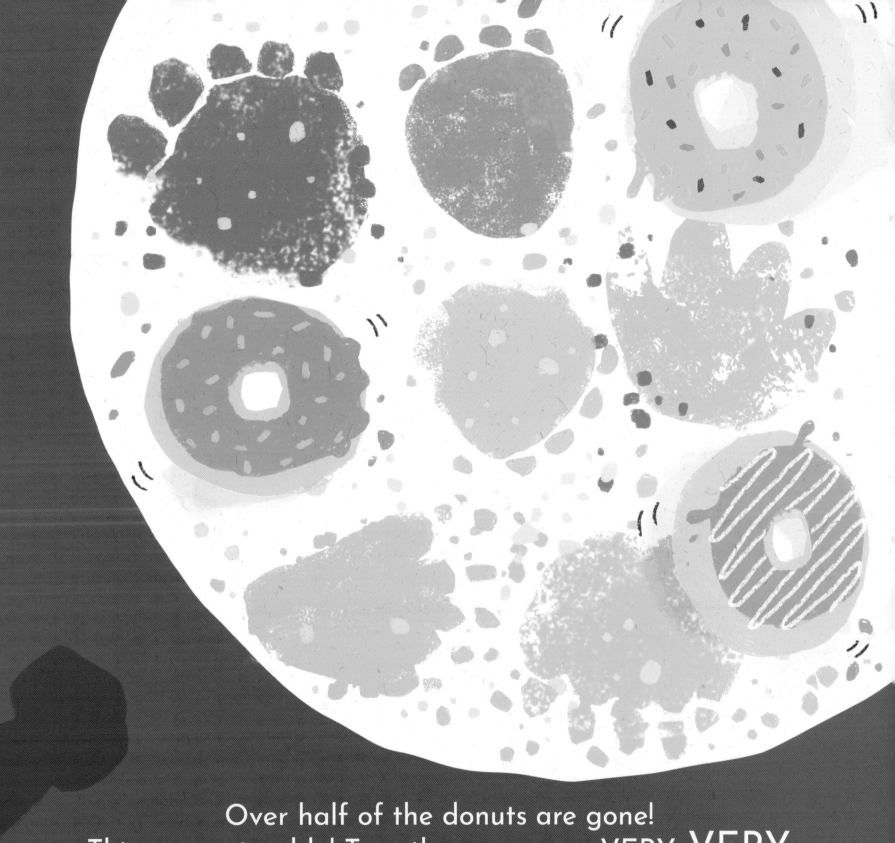

Over half of the donuts are gone!
This means trouble! Turn the page very, VERY, VERY
carefully ... without touching the donuts.

Boo-hoo!
My favourite frosted
donut has **gone!**

Did you touch my donuts?

Keep your
fingers away
from them ...

DO
NOT
TOUCH!

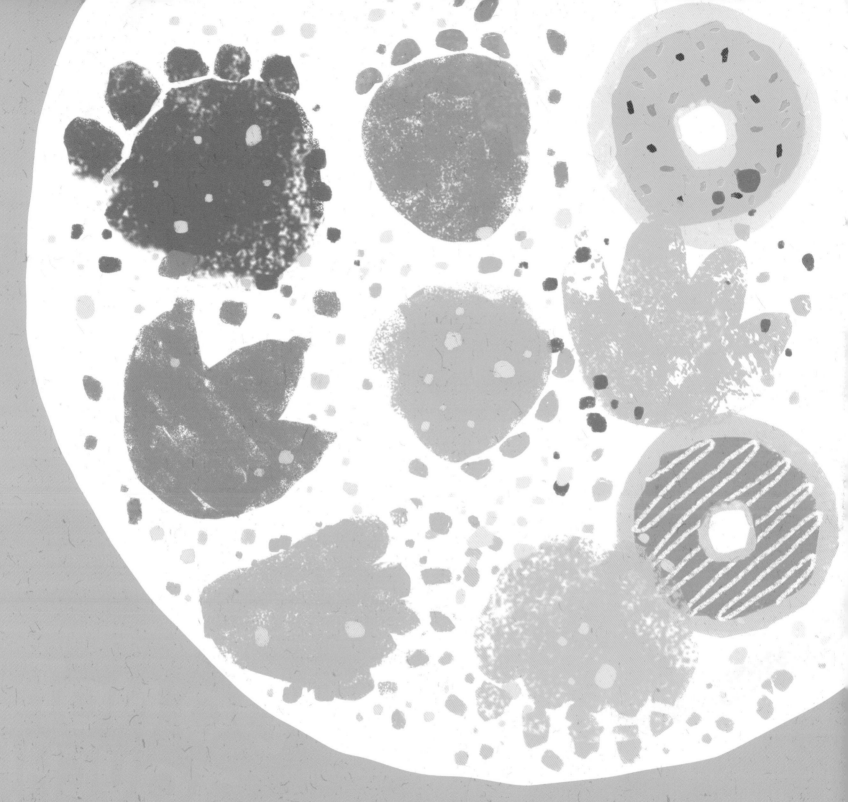

Oh dear! Mikey is really sad!
Turn the page without touching the donuts
and making him more upset.

Gulp! only **ONE** donut is left!

Did you touch my donuts? Keep your fingers away from it ...

DO NOT TOUCH!

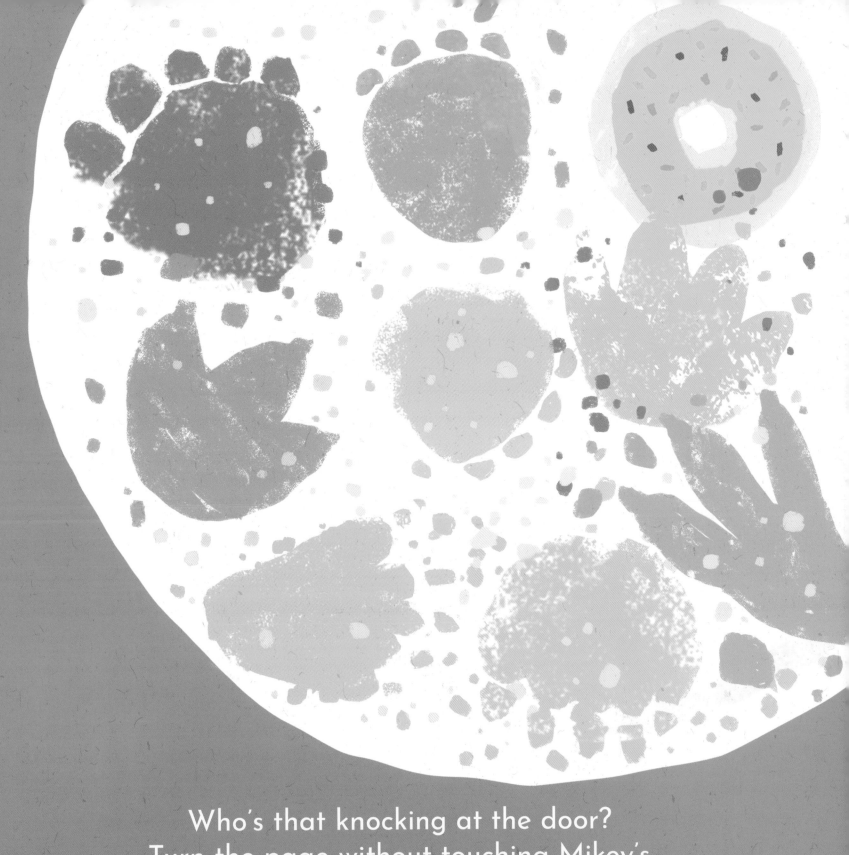

Who's that knocking at the door?
Turn the page without touching Mikey's
very last donut, or the donut-y remains.

Mikey realises that it is good to share.
But just to be sure, turn the page
without touching that donut!

Sorry!
Would **YOU** like to share my last donut?
Use your fingers ...

YOU CAN TOUCH!

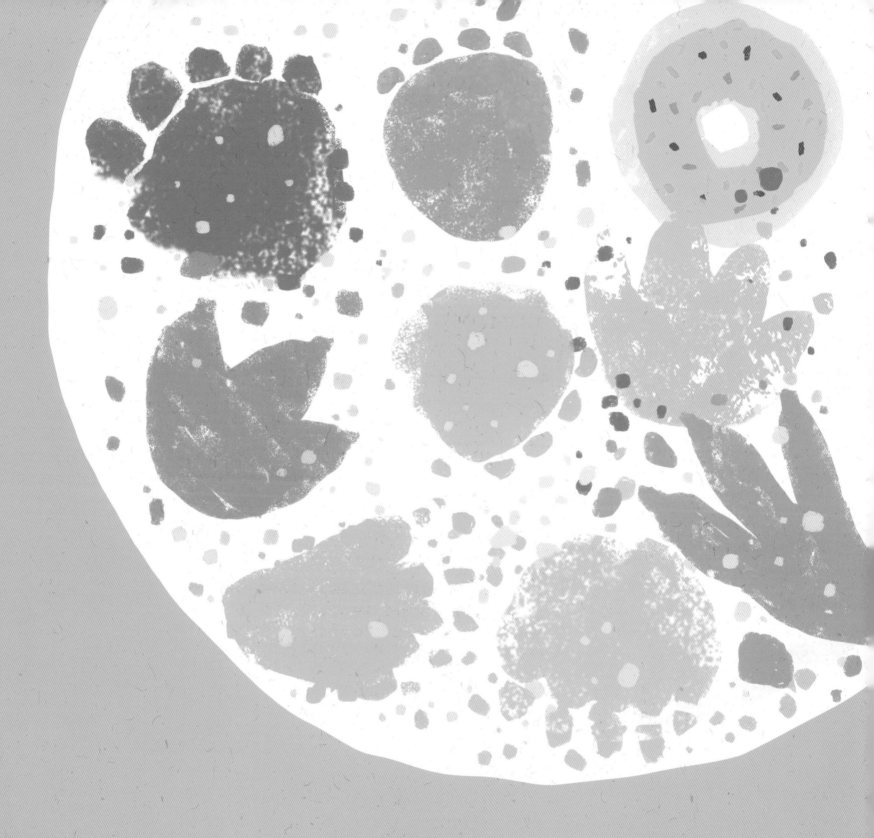

Mikey likes sharing now! Phew!
Turn the page any way you like!

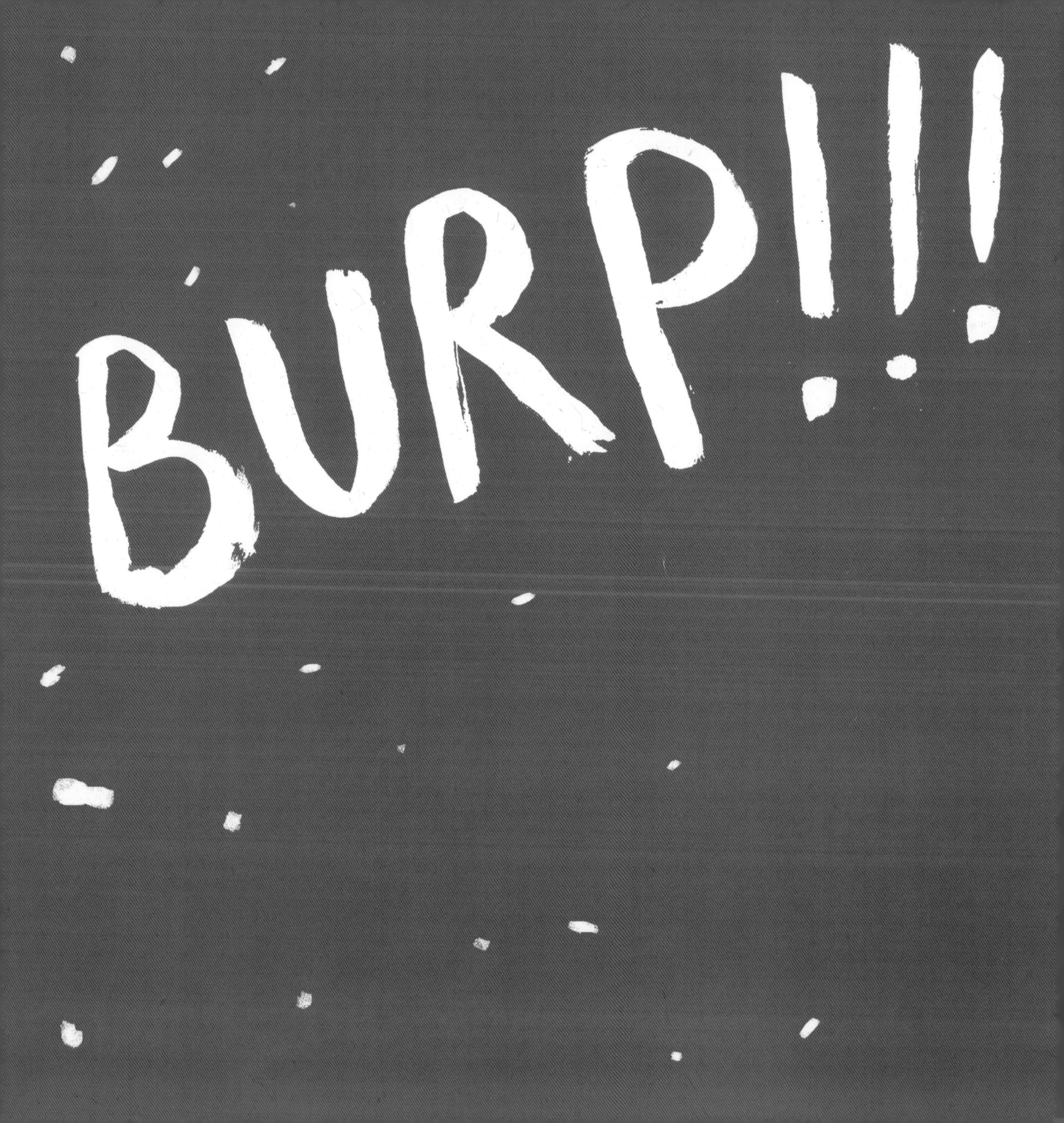
BURP!!!

These donuts are

mine!

Use your fingers to
share them with me!

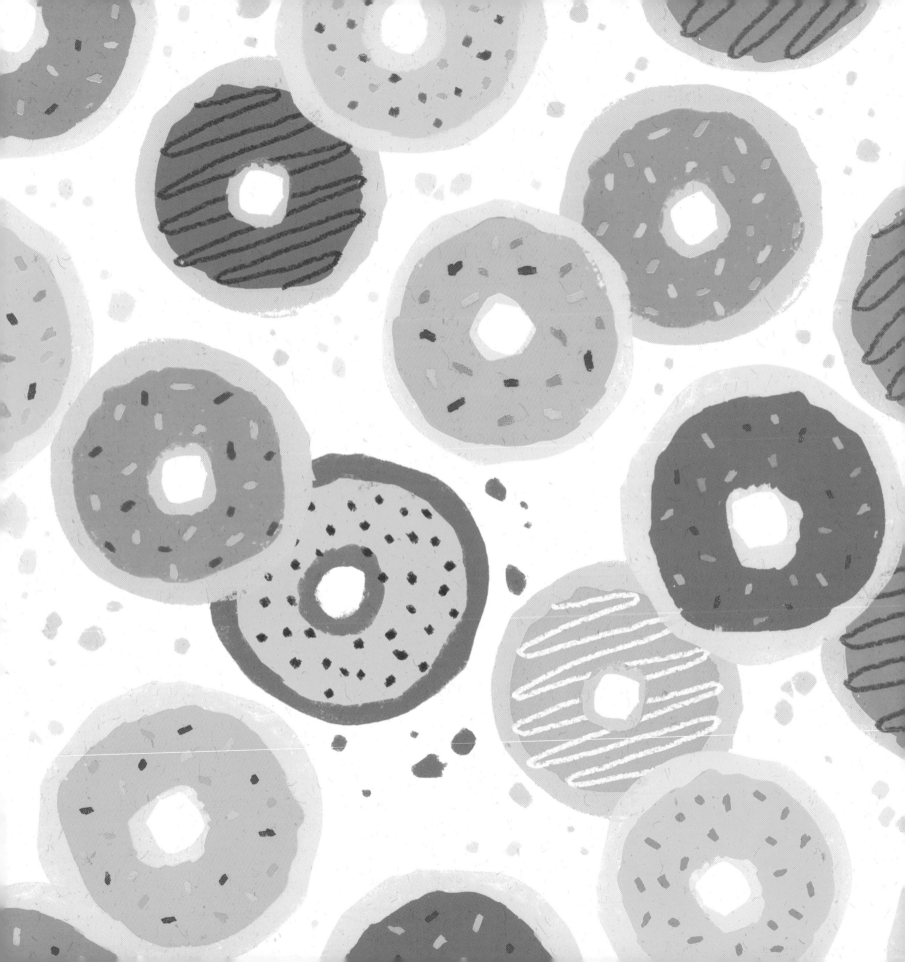

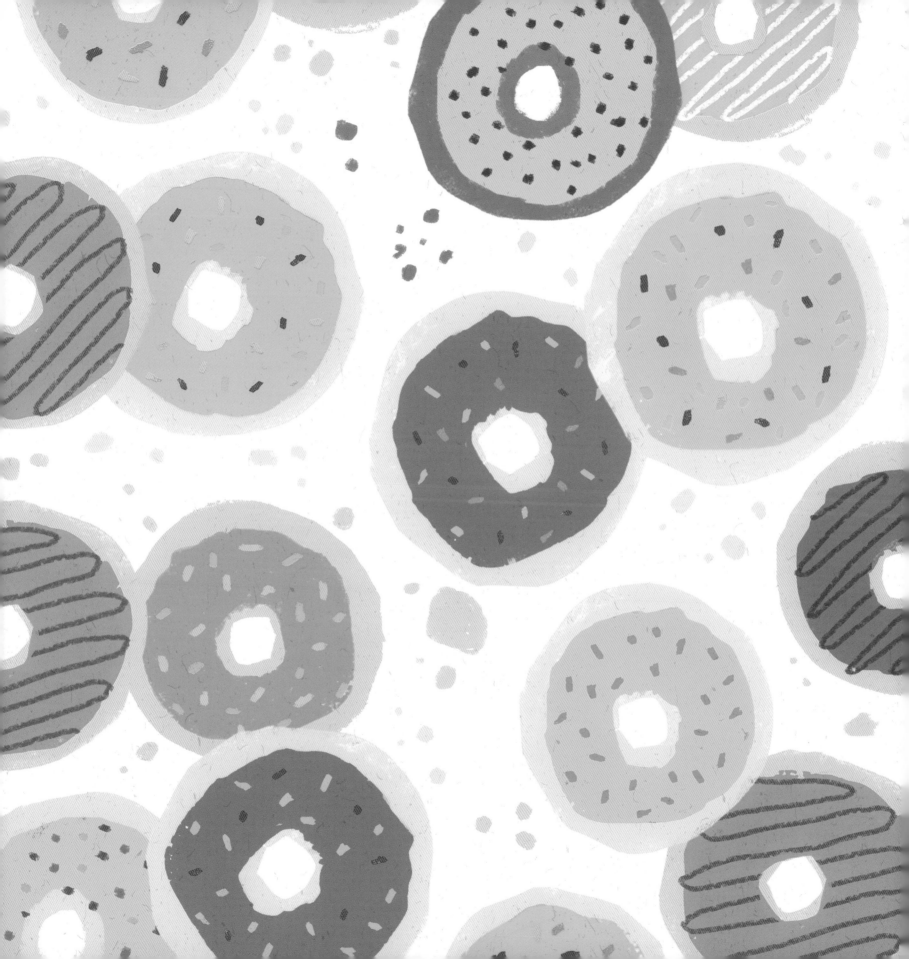